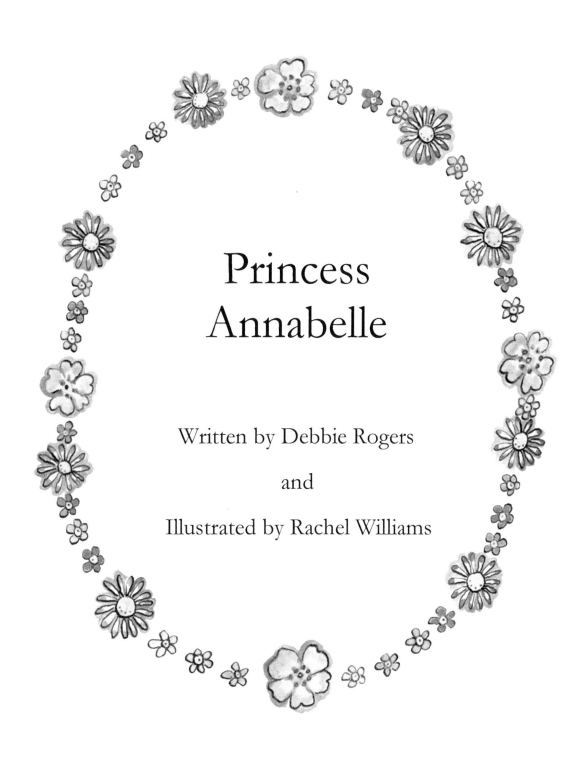

Princess
Annabelle

Written by Debbie Rogers

and

Illustrated by Rachel Williams

LIONESS
WRITING LIMITED

Published by Lioness Writing Ltd
www.lionesswritingltd.com

ISBN: 1999746406
ISBN-13: 978-1-9997464-0-7

DEDICATION

I would like to dedicate this book to my family
and in particular Madeleine, my daughter,
who was really rather like Annabelle.

CONTENTS

ACKNOWLEDGEMENTS

My heartfelt thanks go to Charlotte, who played an important role in getting the book published; also to Richard for his tireless effort checking and re-checking the story and, finally, to Elsa and Mark who have been brave enough to publish it.

Annabelle Sarah Maria Barnes

INTRODUCTION

Annabelle dreamed of being a princess. So Annabelle had to spend a lot of time choosing which sparkly jewels and long, silky dresses to wear; she adored dancing and pirouetting around, pretending she was at splendid parties. Mummy and Daddy both said that she was definitely the most beautiful princess they had ever seen.

But sometimes Annabelle did admit she was really just an ordinary little girl: at bedtime Annabelle did enjoy a cuddle from her quite ordinary Mummy and Daddy. Annabelle was a little unusual in that she had three brothers and one sister, and most of Annabelle's friends had just one brother or sister. They lived in a busy, slightly crowded house with a large garden. Kate was nine: she did not want to be a princess; she wanted to be a cricketer or even a footballer. Sam, aged eleven, was particularly interested in castles, and thought Annabelle's princess dreams were very sweet. Tom, who was six and already a keen footballer, didn't understand why Annabelle wanted to be a princess. Last of all came Archie, who was almost two: now he would have loved to have been a princess himself – but that story comes later.

CHAPTER 1: Annabelle

Annabelle had been a very large baby. She had weighed ten pounds and that really is a big baby! Annabelle looked like she was three months old when she had just been born.

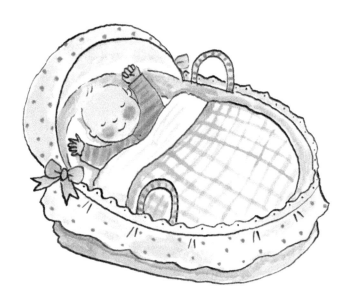

Mrs Barnes, Annabelle's Mum, felt that such a big baby really should have quite a big name. This was just as well since Sam, Annabelle's oldest brother, desperately wanted her to be called Sarah, and Kate definitely preferred the name Maria. So Annabelle's full name was Annabelle Sarah Maria Barnes. This satisfied the whole family!

Now Annabelle, aged four, liked her name very much – she felt princesses were much more likely to have a long name like hers. But Annabelle did have a problem with her name: her family seemed unable to use it. Her oldest brother, Sam, called her Annie, which she found bearable, but he usually went on to call her "NuNu." Now that made her cross! Annabelle couldn't really understand how "NuNu" was even connected with her name. Kate, who liked to play with words, called her "Belle" or "Well" or, worse still, "Belley" or "Welley." Tom, always keen to find a short cut, usually just called her "Boo."

Even her Mummy and Daddy really didn't seem able to get it right. Mummy called her all sorts of names, but very often it was "Annieboo-boo." Daddy had misheard Mummy calling her "Annieboo" and had come up with the interesting name "Naboo."

Annabelle hated "Naboo," she just hated it. It sounded like a strange monster. No princess would ever be called "Naboo." In fact she was very glad that Archie, being so little, couldn't say her name at all and just pointed or shouted at whoever or whatever he wanted.

One Sunday lunch, when Kate had just finished arguing with her brother about whose turn it was to wash up, Annabelle clapped her hands determinedly, flicked her hair behind her ears and asked her family to be quiet. They were all rather stunned and Mummy said, "I think Annabelle has something important to say."

Annabelle looked terribly serious and solemn and announced slowly and clearly, "From now on, I only wish to be called Annabelle."

Her family were bemused and Sam, speaking in a rather grown up voice, expressed the general feeling: "Well Annabelle, that's what we do call you; it's your name, isn't it?" Annabelle narrowed her eyes and tried very, very hard to be patient, but she did sound more than a little exasperated when she replied, with hands on hips, "Of course it's my name, but no-one ever uses it."

Daddy could see that Annabelle was in actual fact close to tears, so very kindly he said, "I think we do call you Annabelle, but we do just now and then like to use a pet name."

It dawned on Annabelle that her family just didn't realise how rarely they used her name. So, loudly and firmly, before anyone else started talking, Annabelle said, "Daddy, you call me Naboo most often; you never call me Annabelle."

"Of course it's my name,
but no-one ever uses it."

Daddy looked slightly hurt: "Don't you like me calling you Naboo?"

Annabelle didn't want to hurt her Daddy's feelings: "I don't like it very much; I'd just like you to call me Annabelle."

At this point Mummy, who had been quite thoughtful, exclaimed, "Do you know I think Annabelle is right! I can't remember when I last called her Annabelle. I think we ought to try and use Annieboo's, I mean Annabelle's, proper name." The family nodded and, policed by Mummy and Daddy, everyone began to try and use Annabelle's proper name. Annabelle would frown sternly when anyone began calling her a pet name, and mostly they stopped and looked repentant.

A whole week went by and Annabelle could not believe how well behaved her family were being – even Tom, who loved teasing, had only whispered "Naboo" at her a couple of times.

Now the trouble came in quite an unexpected way. Annabelle had been practising skipping at Pre-school, and she really was very good at it. Mummy said that she was able to skip like a princess. Daddy said that he was amazed at how dainty she was; that it was definitely princess-like.

Then he sang her a little rhyme:

"Skiperune, Skiperune,

Yes, we know you're not a prune."

Annabelle was terribly proud of her skipping, and Daddy rather enjoyed singing his rhyme. So, over the weekend, there was a whole lot of skipping, nearly always accompanied by Daddy singing his rhyme. Archie in particular seemed to enjoy this and, now he was beginning to talk, he yelled," More, more!" Sam and Tom both finally said that they had had enough of Annabelle's skipping and Daddy's singing, and Mummy even said she could do with a bit of peace. Daddy looked more disappointed than Annabelle and said there would be just one more performance.

Mummy, Sam and Tom visibly relaxed when the final performance ceased, but Archie's face fell. He ran to Daddy, begging, "More, more." Daddy knelt down and kissed him: "Not now Archie, later." But Archie was not satisfied. He ran to Annabelle pleading, "More Prune, Prune."

Tom exploded in laughter. "If Archie can call Annabelle Prune, can I?" Annabelle frowned sternly at Tom, but Archie was very pleased that Tom was laughing at him and shouted, "Prune, Prune!" Annabelle narrowed her eyes: she felt cross with both the boys.

Daddy decided action was needed. He grinned, flung Archie in the air and said:

"Come on Annabelle; you skip and I'll sing one very last time for today:

"Skiperune, Skiperune,

Yes, we know you're not a prune."

Annabelle forgot about being cross and skipped wonderfully. Mummy smiled. "We may occasionally call you names, but we always think of you as our own Princess Annabelle."

CHAPTER 2: Meeting Rosie

"After Pre-school today, we are going round to Toby's house. Won't that be nice Annabelle?" Mummy said, as they arrived at Pre-school.

Annabelle thought for a moment. "No! He plays fighting games or trains and I don't want to go." She narrowed her eyes.

Gently but firmly, Mummy stated, "We are going to Toby's house and I am sure you will enjoy it."

Annabelle looked a bit sulky, but she didn't really mind: she loved going to other people's houses and maybe she could persuade Toby to be a king while she was a princess.

After Pre-school, they walked round the corner to Toby's. Archie was very excited: he loved exploring new places and he knew Toby's tall, red-brick house was full of boys' toys.

When they arrived, Toby was playing with his action figures – Annabelle did not think this looked too hopeful. But, to her surprise, Archie was actually quite helpful: he was so excited at seeing the fighting men spread over the floor that he kept grabbing them, so Toby was quite willing to play something else.

Annabelle was so patient, explaining that Toby could be either a king or a pirate, but he would keep having ideas of his own. (Imagine thinking he could be Superman in a princess game.) Annabelle was about to be very firm with Toby when the doorbell rang and another lady with a little girl arrived. The little girl had blonde hair, like Annabelle's, but, unlike Annabelle's hair, it was beautifully curly. Rosie beamed at Annabelle and ignored poor Toby. Rosie wore a shiny blue Cinderella dress and certainly looked ready to play princesses.

Rosie and Annabelle smiled at each other. Rosie understood that Toby had to be a prince, "And we will be the most beautiful princesses in the world!"

Over lunch, Annabelle and Rosie sat next to each other and Toby sat next to Archie. It was Toby's favourite meal: pasta with bacon and sweetcorn, with lots of cheese to go over the top. Annabelle flicked her hair behind her ears, to avoid dipping it in the pasta sauce, and grinned: "This is wonderful food, just right for princesses and princes." And Archie obviously agreed. He kept trying to pinch food from everybody else's plates.

Lunch was eaten pretty quickly, as everyone realised that that was the easiest way to stop Archie grabbing their food. Just before whisking her yoghurt away from Archie, Rosie declared that there was going to be a Princess Ball that afternoon. Of course, Annabelle adored this idea and shouted (in a slightly unprincess-like way), "We'll dance so amazingly! Toby will be begging to marry us both, but we won't bother marrying him."

Rosie instantly understood. "Of course we can't marry Toby He's going to be an ugly, wicked prince." The girls nodded in agreement.

Toby pulled a hideous face: he was definitely not going to be a prince and he was beginning to think he didn't like girls anyway. Fortunately, Archie didn't mind being an ugly prince, and he liked the idea of dancing with the girls at the ball. Though, unfortunately, Archie's idea of dancing really meant chasing the girls and saying, "Marr' me!" Meanwhile, Toby was happy: he ignored his guests and played with his action figures.

All too soon, the afternoon's play came to an end: all the mummies had older children to pick up from school. But, the next day, Annabelle could talk of nothing but Rosie. She put her hands out dramatically: "Do you know Mummy, I really, really like Rosie? Rosie is so pretty; could she come and play, please, please?"

Mummy did not commit herself too quickly: "Well probably, sometime soon." It had to be admitted that Mummy was slightly concerned that, while all Annabelle could think and talk about was Rosie, it was quite possible that Rosie might not think very much about Annabelle again.

The next day, they bumped into Rosie and her mum. Rosie grinned excitedly at Annabelle, jigging up and down on the spot, tugging at her mummy's hand. Rosie's mummy smiled, "Okay, okay. Rosie absolutely loved playing with Annabelle. Could Annabelle come and play on Friday?"

Annabelle was nodding her head and smiling effervescently. Mrs. Barnes grinned and said, "You have just made Annabelle's day; she would love to come and play." Annabelle was fizzing with excitement!

Playing at princesses at Rosie's house was wonderful and now she looked forward to Pre-school more than ever because Rosie was there too. They walked around together holding hands; they did paintings at the same time, and sticking at the same time, and they always sat next to each other when it came to snack time.

Rosie confided in Annabelle, after they had eaten their pieces of fruit during snack time: "Annabelle, you are my bestest friend ever."

Annabelle squeezed Rosie's hand and gave a massive smile: "You are my bestest friend too."

When mummy picked Annabelle up, Annabelle asked mummy, "Can you guess who my best friend is?"

Mummy looked thoughtful. "Maybe Monica or Emily, or Tony."

Annabelle jumped up and down, "No, No!" Then she smiled radiantly and announced: "Rosie is my best ever friend."

"I just wouldn't have guessed!" Mummy gave Annabelle a great big hug: "Do you know, I think it might be a great idea if we invited Rosie round for lunch!"

CHAPTER 3: Archie Tries To Be a Princess

Archie had beautiful hair, really beautiful – the sort of hair any princess would adore having. Archie, almost two, had lovely long golden curls. Annabelle loved to play with his hair, using ribbons for pony tails and bunches and all sorts of strange styles.

Both Sam and Tom were thoroughly embarrassed by Archie's hair, especially when old ladies stopped to admire him, "Doesn't she look like a little angel. I bet she's good."

Tom, who played a lot of football and only ever played with boys at school, complained that some of his friends wouldn't even believe that Archie was a boy. Archie didn't care. He liked all the attention Annabelle gave him doing his hair. Mummy also loved his curls and just couldn't bring herself to cut his hair yet.

One morning, looking in the large, old fashioned wardrobe in her bedroom, Annabelle explained, "Rosie and I need all the most beautiful things because we will be princesses."

Certain that Annabelle needed his help, Archie kept tugging at scarves and dresses. He was enjoying himself: there were shiny dresses, and colourful necklaces and glittery things everywhere. He jumped up and down and tried to catch Annabelle's attention, crying out, "Me, me!" Annabelle was not listening: princesses had so much to think about.

When Rosie finally arrived, both Annabelle and Archie were so excited: "You have to come upstairs this minute; we will be so, so beautiful; I have found all the very prettiest dresses and things for us."

Rosie was suitably amazed. "Wow, we can be incredible princesses!"

Leaping around Rosie, Archie pleaded, "Me, me."

Annabelle tried to be patient; she was fond of Archie. "You can play if you're a good boy."

Meanwhile, Rosie was selecting a dress and jewels. Archie determinedly grabbed Rosie's dress and necklace. Rosie laughed. "You can't be a princess, you're only a boy."

Archie wailed loudly, "Mee, meeee."

Feeling a little worried that Archie would spoil this special time with Rosie, Annabelle tried her best to please Archie so that she and Rosie could play: "Let's just let him have that dress. Look Rosie, this one is much prettier."

Yet once the girls had helped him into one dress, he wanted another dress on top of it, as well as pointing determinedly at the beads Rosie was looking at. When Rosie picked up a velvet skirt, he screamed; when she picked up a handbag, he grabbed that. Annabelle had three crowns: Archie attempted to wear all three, plus two pretty, floaty scarves.

Annabelle felt desperate: so far, neither she nor Rosie had been able to dress up at all. Just then, Mummy popped her head round the door. "Is everything alright?"

Annabelle explained, "Archie wants everything – we just can't do anything."

Rosie joined in: "Archie keeps taking my dresses and my jewels."

Poor Archie looked quite a sight with layers of princess clothing on his sturdy little body. Archie thought he looked quite beautiful, and pleaded, with tears in his eyes, "Me prince." Mummy felt very sorry for Archie, but she did see that he was being impossible. Rosie and Annabelle were never going to be able to play, with Archie stubbornly grabbing anything pretty that caught his fancy. By now both Annabelle and Archie looked tearful.

Mummy gave Archie a big cuddle and said, "With your lovely hair, you do look a bit like a princess, but I think we must give Annabelle and Rosie the chance to play." Then poor Mummy had quite a struggle getting the clothes off Archie. He screamed and kicked, but finally she carried him downstairs, minus princess accessories, sweaty and glowing.

Peace reigned upstairs and Mummy, as a special treat, let the girls eat their fruit on the sofa in Annabelle's bedroom (normally children were not allowed to eat upstairs).

The girls dressed themselves and were actually able to play without interference. When it came to lunchtime, Archie was looking very pleased with himself. Annabelle was intrigued. "What did Archie do, mummy?"

Mummy smiled and said, "Archie may not make a perfect princess, but he is very good at helping to make princess chocolate cakes. Even if his hair does become a little chocolatey."

Rosie and Annabelle grinned and said, "Can we have some princess cake?"

Archie nodded. He was very proud of himself. He giggled. "Not eat hair." Archie waved his chocolate-covered curls in front of the girls, who both giggled with him.

CHAPTER 4: Mistakes

It was Mrs Turnbull's birthday. Mrs Turnbull was the old lady who lived next door to the Barnes family. She loved children, and was slightly deaf, so she was never disturbed, no matter how noisy the Barnes family were. Mummy always said this was a great blessing. Another reason she was a popular neighbour was that she always remembered to give a little gift on the children's birthdays. So Mummy had said that, now it was Mrs Turnbull's birthday, Archie and Annabelle should each make a card for her.

Annabelle and Archie were a little reluctant to make a card. It would interrupt playing Mummies and babies: it was a lot of fun, with Archie crawling around as a baby, but when Archie crawled over Annabelle's foot she decided a change might be good: "Okay Mummy, I'll do a really pretty sticking-picture with shiny paper, sequins and glitter." Annabelle enjoyed creating wonderful pictures and was now full of ideas. She carefully drew a princess and began sticking various materials onto the beautiful dress.

Seeing all the splendid shiny things that Annabelle had before her, Archie couldn't wait to get started. Excitedly he jumped up and down, grabbing at shiny things, crying, "Me, me." Sequins went flying in all directions.

Mummy dived towards Archie, catching hold of his arm before Annabelle's picture was ruined. Then, coaxingly, Mummy said, "Why don't you sit at the other end of the table and I'll get you your own shiny things, and you can even have your own glue."

Smiling broadly, Archie was satisfied and ran round to the other end of the table and clambered up onto a chair. Mummy selected some shiny things: "Look Archie. See how Mummy is spreading the glue." Unfortunately, Archie was not very patient when he was feeling artistic, and he was definitely not the sort of boy to waste time listening to instructions. He screeched, "Mine," and at the same time grabbed the glue spreader, spattering Mummy with drips of glue. Archie was undaunted and began smearing vast amounts of glue all over the card.

Mummy looked stressed and muttered, "I can't believe I

suggested this." Archie grinned and proceeded to plaster the paper with more and more glue.

"Dring, dring!"- Mummy rushed to the phone.

As Mummy chatted on the phone, Archie continued to layer glue on his card and glue was now dripping onto the table and floor. Finally, Annabelle glanced over at Archie: she felt, in fact she knew, something had to be done. Annabelle frowned, put her hands on her hips, and said in a very superior voice, "Look Archie, there really is too much glue on that picture. I will have to take some of the glue off it."

Archie pulled a particularly stubborn face and shouted, "No! No! Mine!"

Frowning sternly at Archie, Annabelle marched to the other end of the table and grabbed Archie's picture.

This was perhaps not such a good idea. Glue dripped in a wide circle over and around Archie. Archie screeched. Appalled at the attack on his work of art, he threw a piece of very sticky shiny paper at Annabelle. It stuck to Annabelle's face and Archie quite forgot his tantrum and roared with laughter: "Silly Belle, silly, silly."

Annabelle grinned, pulled the paper off her face, then said persuasively, "Put the paper on your picture, not on my nose you Silly." Archie smiled sweetly: he had again begun to focus on the wonderful shiny things before him. There was a definite gleam in his eyes as glitter, sequins and shiny paper were piled up and pressed onto the picture. Annabelle watched in fascination: there was a marked contrast between the two cards.

Mummy returned. The kitchen floor was covered with glue and sequins. There was a moment of paralysis, while Mummy took stock of the chaos. Then, very calmly, and in a particularly controlled tone, Mummy told the children to go upstairs and play while she cleared up the mess.

Wailing in protest, Archie shook his head: he did not like to have to change his plans, especially when he was feeling creative. But Annabelle could see that Mummy had really had enough. She took Archie's hand and coaxed: "Come on Archie; let's go and play dressing up. Mummy is really cross now. Let's go upstairs."

Once upstairs, Annabelle realized quite what a state Archie was in. There was glue and glitter all over him. Annabelle wanted to help Mummy, and she felt Mummy would be so pleased if she sorted Archie out – cleaned and tidied him. First of all, Annabelle helped Archie wash his hands, arms and face. Then she noticed how much glue was in his hair, and explained in a very grown up voice that she would have to sort out his hair as well. She tried to wash it out with a damp sponge, but somehow that just seemed to spread it through Archie's golden curls.

The challenge of sorting out Archie's hair was becoming pretty absorbing, for Annabelle really wanted to get him looking decent before Mummy came upstairs. Next, Annabelle attempted to brush the glue out of Archie's hair.

Archie did not enjoy this and yelled, "No, no, no, no!" He even attempted to run away from his sister. Nevertheless, Annabelle was still determined to help Mummy, and sort out Archie's hair. It was then that she noticed that Archie's hair was becoming matted and so concluded that more drastic measures were called for.

Annabelle put on her best grown-up voice and said very calmly, "Do stop being a baby and making all this fuss. I shall just cut the sticky bits out of your hair."

Enthusiastically Archie yelled, "Yes, yes, yessie, yes!" He looked so delighted that Annabelle felt sure this was a good idea. Confidently, Annabelle grabbed the pair of scissors on her bedroom floor and in no time at all there was the sound of snipping.

As we all know, it is not easy to cut anyone's hair if they will just not keep still, and Archie was very excited and just could not stop jigging around. Annabelle had not cut hair before and continued snipping in spite of Archie's wriggling. The result was a MESS! A big MESS!

Snip Snip

All of a sudden, Annabelle understood just what she had done. It was Annabelle's turn to scream. Mummy came running upstairs to see Annabelle sobbing on the floor, scissors in hand, while Archie gazed at his own reflection in the wardrobe mirror. He beamed joyously when he saw his Mummy and announced, "Archie smart boy!"

There was a look of horror on Mummy's face and then she sat down on the floor with an arm round each of the children and began laughing. Annabelle was definitely confused; Archie grinned: "Mummy loves hair." Annabelle shook her head in disbelief: Archie had long and short tufts all over his head and, giggling nervously, she whispered, "Maybe it is a bit funny."

CHAPTER 5: Smar' Archie

Storms of laughter greeted Daddy, Sam, Tom and Kate on their return from school. They thundered upstairs. Sam looked appalled; Tom sniggered; Kate grinned and exclaimed, "Archie doesn't look like a girl any more, he just looks weird!"

Annabelle looked desperately at Daddy; tears were beginning to trickle down her face as the enormity of her crime began to sink in: "I just wanted to help......now Archie has lost his beautiful curls. He looks horrible and ugly and it's all my fault. I'm so sorry."

Daddy smiled broadly and said, "I don't think Archie minds a bit; look at him." Indeed, Archie was having a splendid time kicking around the golden curls on the floor, without a care in the world. Mummy picked Annabelle up and said, "Archie could never look horrible."

Daddy cleared up the mess on the floor, then announced, "Time for haircut number two, Archie. I'll just get my special scissors. I think I'll do this haircut, Annabelle, unless you fancy another go." Annabelle shook her head very firmly. "I never, ever want to touch a pair of scissors again." But she couldn't help giggling when Archie begged, "Annie cut me! I like!"

Before any haircuts, Daddy made Mummy a relaxing cup of tea in the living room, and gave the children juice and biscuits in the kitchen. Then Daddy told Sam and Kate that they were in charge and that they must try and keep

Annabelle and Archie out of trouble for just five minutes while Mummy enjoyed some peace and quiet.

As the oldest child in the family, Sam felt it was his job to cheer Annabelle up, so he picked her up, then swung her round: "It's fantastic! Archie will finally look like a boy." Just to show how happy he was, he thrust the last biscuit at Annabelle and said, "Go on Annie; you deserve the last biscuit." Archie was also very happy, despite having knocked over two glasses of juice. Tom stated that he might be able to play football without all that girly hair.

Drinks and biscuits finished, Daddy carefully sat Archie in the high chair and explained, "Archie you will have to sit very still. Could you do that for Daddy? Then Daddy can give you a big boy's haircut."

Archie looked rather solemn, nodded his head and said, "Smar' Archie." Archie was definitely enjoying the attention.

Somehow or other, Archie managed to remain pretty still for about half an hour, while his remaining curls fell to the ground. Annabelle's eyes followed each curl as it dropped to the floor. She picked up each sticky bit of hair, for it seemed such a shame to throw the glue-covered golden curls in the bin.

Happily, Archie was thrilled with his new haircut and he was also very proud of the card he had made for Mrs Turnbull. Kate kindly cleaned off the excess glue; she and Annabelle couldn't stop giggling when they realized how heavy Archie's card was with the layers of glue, glitter, sequins and shiny paper. Their little brother just grinned:

"Arch pu' lots shiny on!"

"Before everything falls off that card, we had better pop next door, Archie, "Mummy gasped.

Fortunately, Mrs Turnbull knew just what to say when Archie arrived: "Who is this handsome young man?" Archie jumped up and down, saying, "Archie smar' boy," and then gave Mrs Turnbull a great big, sticky kiss.

Their lovely neighbour was so appreciative: "Princess cards are a real favourite of mine and your card is very special Archie; it really is quite heavy with all you have stuck

onto it." Archie beamed.

Meanwhile, back at home, Annabelle had been busy: she

was just finishing off when Mummy entered the kitchen

only to find Annabelle in action with the glue. This was a

bit too much for Mummy who gasped, "Oh no! I just can't

cope with more mess."

Annabelle grinned "It's okay Mummy. I've finished.

Look! It's a picture of Archie with his long curls. I stuck his hair on my picture of him so you'll always remember Archie with long hair."

Mummy smiled. "Wow! That is a fantastic picture; I really will treasure it. I only hope the hair doesn't fall off."

Kate, who was always quite practical, solved the problem "I'll put sticky back plastic on the picture so the hair will stay there forever." Mummy looked relieved that the hair wouldn't be dropping off all over the place; she had had enough mess for one day. She picked Annabelle up and kissed her: "Well, what a day and what marvelously clever girls I have!"

CHAPTER 6: Daddy Goes Climbing

Mummy and Daddy were having some old friends round to dinner. This meant that Saturday, during the day, was probably going to be a bit grim for everyone: the family had to TIDY!

The Barnes family lived in a fairly big house: Mummy and Daddy had a bedroom; Sam and Tom shared a room which was cluttered with books and action figures; Kate had her own tidy little room; Annabelle shared with Archie. She tried to insist on a clear line down the middle so that Archie's cuddly toys didn't spill into the princess side of the room.

Only Daddy and Kate were tidy people, so clothes, toys and books seemed to spread themselves over the house. "This house looks as though a tornado has hit it," Daddy moaned.

Mummy complained in a loud, slightly threatening voice, "Nobody ever puts anything away – there are heaps of everybody's stuff all over the kitchen."

The children were unusually quiet; they dreaded the inevitable call to chores. Yet it came: Daddy announced, "Mummy and I cannot do all the work in this family; you are all going to help. Do you hear?"

The four children sat in sullen silence. Tom was mumbling a vague sort of tune to the words, "Mess, mess, mess, there is a mess, mess, mess…"

"You're quite right, Tom, but we are going to do something about it. Annabelle, Tom, all toys upstairs; Kate, hoovering; Sam, washing up.

Moans rang through the house, but the children accepted their inevitable jobs. Annabelle was not good at tidying: she was a very imaginative child and each toy seemed to spark a little story in her mind and she'd just somehow end up playing with it. Mummy was not pleased when she caught Annabelle building a climbing frame for her dolls out of Archie's bricks. Daddy frowned sternly when he saw her playing libraries. Mummy finally said, "Annabelle, could you just take Archie out into the garden, so neither of you can make any further mess." Annabelle was delighted; Kate grumbled that it was "sooo unfair," but Annabelle had quickly escaped.

Out in the garden, Annabelle and Archie played on the see-saw, then kicked lots of leaves around. The Barnes' garden was rather unusual; it was like a piece of mini woodland, so there were an awful lot of leaves around.

The leaves swirled high and low as the children attacked them. Unfortunately, poor Archie got some mud kicked in his eye. So, Annabelle made a suggestion: "Let's make beds for ourselves out of the leaves." Archie toppled backwards onto his bed, while Annabelle tucked herself into the leaves with the greatest of care; but both children were soon extremely muddy and disheveled.

Meanwhile, Mummy and Daddy had deemed that the house was now acceptably tidy. Sam, Tom and Kate rushed outside to avoid any further jobs and ran into Archie and Annabelle. "Oh, no; you two look like scarecrows!" Kate gasped when she saw them.

Archie jumped up and down and shouted, "Me bed, me bed." Annabelle was a little embarrassed now, and made a rather feeble attempt to get leaves from her jumper.

"Never mind, Annie, it was a good idea making leaf beds, but let's play hide-and-seek," Sam said sympathetically. Sam loved organizing his younger siblings, though Kate, who was only just two years younger than him, was often not easily organized. "I'm counting to a hundred," Sam shouted authoritatively and began counting quickly. "One, two, three…" The other children scattered and Tom, pulling a rather giggly face, dragged Archie after him.

Knowing her brother's weaknesses, Kate ran to the back of the garden, weighing up which tree she would climb. Sam was not sporty like Kate and there was no way he would be able to climb up the tree and catch her.

When Sam had counted to fifty, Kate was already nearing the top of the tree. Annabelle, knowing how brilliant Kate was at hiding, had followed her and now she too was climbing the tree.

"Go down, Annabelle – you're too high, it's not safe!" Kate whispered in a slightly panicky voice.

"Seventy-one, seventy-two," Sam yelled.

"I just can't: Sam will find me," Annabelle replied. Annabelle was a confident climber and was determined to be well out of Sam's reach. At almost twenty feet up the tree, Annabelle began to feel less sure of herself. She shouted to Kate but her voice began to trail off as she realised her feet were slipping towards the end of the branch which was bending under her weight. Annabelle's hands stung as she frantically clung to the branch as tightly as she could.

In absolute terror Annabelle whimpered, but fortunately Kate's reactions were somewhat more extreme. She scrambled down the tree at a double quick speed, yelling wildly, "It's Annie, it's Annie – she'll fall! Get Daddy, get Daddy."

Daddy raced to the back of the garden. He turned pale as he jerked his head back to glimpse Annabelle clinging onto a slender branch. Then, trying very hard to sound calm, he shouted, "Annabelle, you just hold on tight. Daddy's coming."

Annabelle whimpered, "Daddy, Daddy, I think I'm slipping." Daddy climbed so quickly, he literally shot up the tree. Tom wildly yelled, "She's going to fall!" Archie began to scream in terror. Annabelle was now at the very end of the branch. Daddy somehow managed to reach a branch which he could stand on: he was just beginning to reach towards Annabelle when she screamed. She was now dangling, clinging to the branch with just one hand.

Daddy, carefully balanced, cried out, "Hang on Angel!" Just as Annabelle knew she couldn't hold on a second longer, Daddy's hand grabbed her trousers around the waist. Daddy's voice was still hoarse as he said, "It's alright – I've got you now." Seconds later they were on firm ground again.

"Sor..Sorry Daddy, I knew I shouldn't have gone so high," Annabelle said quietly with tears in her eyes.

Daddy was ashen and he replied very firmly, "You must never climb that tree again – do you hear me?" Annabelle nodded; she felt very sorry she had given everyone such a fright.

Archie, Tom and Kate hugged them. Tom pointed out, "I wasn't properly found, so I'm not counting this time. Annie should count, then she can't climb any more trees."

Daddy laughed. "I don't know about Annabelle, but I need coffee and cake!"

Annabelle grinned and said, "Cake, then counting." Everyone seemed to agree with Annabelle, and in just a few minutes Mummy was handing round slices of lemon cake.

CHAPTER 7: CHAOS

"Mummy, I need trainers for Monday!" Kate announced. Mummy sighed. "Why are you letting me know on Saturday morning? The last thing I want to do is spend my Saturday trekking round crowded shops." Kate was a forceful character and just re-asserted, "I need the trainers Mummy."

A couple of hours later, Mummy was in town with four out of the five children. Sam had gone round to a friend's house and Daddy had had to go into work. Tom was quite pleased to be in town, as he had some birthday money to spend. Kate was purposeful, suggesting all the possible places to buy trainers. Annabelle and Archie were miserable; both sensed a long drag around town.

First the family headed for a toy shop so Tom could spend his money. Annabelle was keen to look at dolls. There was a particularly beautiful doll with gorgeous princess clothes.

Unfortunately for Annabelle, Mummy held her hand tightly and said, "Sorry Angel, we'll have to stick together, it's just too crowded to see everything." Annabelle narrowed her eyes grumpily at Mummy who did not even seem to notice, as she was concentrating on pushing Archie's buggy away from the cuddly cat he was attempting to grab.

Tom boldly led the way to the construction toys and grabbed a massive, shimmering box – Mummy shook her head and Tom reluctantly selected a much smaller packet of Lego, more suited to his budget. Thinking that they were now going to be able to make a quick retreat, Mummy was pleased.

It was Kate, always so alert, who noticed that Archie was missing.

Desperately, the family scanned the sea of people around them, but there was no Archie. "Where on earth could he have got to?" Mummy groaned. She sighed: "Let's all keep together and look through the shop." What with people and toys everywhere, it was not easy to search for one small boy.

Mummy was obviously worried. Annabelle, very fond of Archie, imagined how frightened he might be and quietly sobbed. "What if we don't find him?" Archie was a pain at times, but Annabelle couldn't bear the thought of losing him. Her imagination had already extended to images of wild beasts carrying him away. But Mummy smiled reassuringly: "Archie will be somewhere here – would Archie leave a toy shop without a big fuss?"

Fifteen minutes of uproar followed: boxes were overturned, shelves ransacked and the shop resounded with shouts of "Archie!" from shop assistants and other customers who had never even met Archie. Mummy was beginning to feel very anxious, and was beginning to wonder if Archie had left the shop. Annabelle felt tense and tight all over, as though she had to do something quickly, but what should she do? She knew there were all sorts of dangers for Archie if they didn't find him quickly.

Then, quite suddenly, she turned to Mummy and yelled above all the hubbub, "It's alright, a monster can't have taken Archie: monsters are huge; we'd have seen a monster." Mummy looked blankly at Annabelle and, strangely, did not seem less worried. Then Annabelle had a real brainwave: "Archie wanted the cat. I know he did!"

Mummy grabbed Annabelle's hand and they raced over to the cuddly toys. There was no obvious sign of Archie, but Annabelle noticed a couple of bears pushed over on one particularly deep shelf and right at the back, wedged behind a particularly ferocious looking lion was Archie! Annabelle bravely pushed the lion to one side and there was Archie very happily playing with a gorgeously fluffy white cat.

Archie grinned and held the cat tightly to his chest and said, "Mine!" Annabelle yelled, "He's here, he's here!" She gave him a tight hug, but thought she'd like to thump him as well; he had been so naughty!

Mummy hugged them both and whispered in Annabelle's ear, "You're fantastic. I don't think we'd ever have found him without you." Then, in quite a stern voice, Mummy asked Archie why he had hidden and not come out when so many people were calling his name.

Archie hugged the fluffy cat and said a little sorrowfully, "Mine, play mine." Mummy and Annabelle looked at each other. They understood Archie's logic pretty well – he had been desperate to play with the toy cat and had felt the only way to manage this was to hide away and just ignore everyone else.

Abruptly, Kate and Tom arrived on the scene. They were both thrilled to see Archie safe and sound, but Kate was keen to make a move and get the trainers, so she made a big mistake and attempted to snatch the fluffy cat from Archie. Outraged, Archie howled loudly; this horendous noise echoed around the shop. Anxiously, the shop manager approached. "Is the little boy hurt?" Mummy swiftly reassured him that Archie was fine and that he just didn't want to put the cuddly toy back.

Behind Mummy, Archie began to sob loudly, "Mine ca', mine ca'." The poor shop manager had had a terrible morning and just wanted his shop back to normal; he was not finding it easy to cope with the steadily increasing wail from Archie, so he smiled indulgently and said, "Well, well the poor wee chap has had quite an ordeal. On behalf of The Great Toys Store I would like to present Archie with that wonderful, cuddly cat."

The crowd of concerned shoppers and shop assistants cheered and clapped: Mummy, Annabelle, Kate and Tom were very embarrassed, but Archie stood up, grinned and waved his cat, shouting, "Arch hap! Arch ha!"

Annabelle couldn't help feeling a bit jealous and felt that action was definitely required: she produced one of her best sulky faces, with narrowed eyes and lips drawn into a very straight line. It was an excellent sulky face and Annabelle was rather peeved that, again, Mummy didn't even notice it. Poor Mummy was far too busy thanking the manager and all the other twenty or so people who had been involved in the search for Archie.

Annabelle tugged at her Mummy and whined, "Please, please could I just have a tiny quick peep at the beautiful princess doll." Mummy rolled her eyes and gasped, "Annie, I just can't believe you're asking that!" Annabelle muttered, "But everybody else is getting something."

Kate looked at Mummy and said, "This has been sooo embarrassing, I think I can wait for my trainers. I never want to come shopping with Archie again."

Mummy laughed. "Archie does seem to cause chaos wherever he goes – but home sounds like a wonderful idea."

Triumphantly, Archie grinned and gloated, "Mine ca', mine ca'." Tom giggled and said, "Okay Archie."

Annabelle couldn't help laughing. "Do you think if I hid for ages in the toy shop, the manager might give me the princess doll?" Mummy narrowed her eyes and threatened, "Don't you dare try it! I don't think the manager will keep giving away toys to members of our family." Annabelle gave a mischievous grin.

CHAPTER 8: Two Lions

One disaster of a shopping trip was quite sufficient for Mummy, so this time Mummy refused to take Archie with her into town. Daddy said all the boys could stay with him and play football.

Tom cheered, "Football is so much more fun than shopping!"

Remembering the previous shopping trip, Daddy felt the girls deserved a treat and suggested, "Why not try out that new coffee shop, with those delicious-looking cakes?"

Annabelle liked this idea and excitedly asked, "Please, please can I have one of those delicious chocolate milkshakes as well?" Mummy nodded, then whispered, "Well just this once but let's get going before Daddy changes his mind."

As well as looking forward to the chocolate drink, Annabelle was hoping desperately that Mummy would go into The Great Toy Store and let her gaze at the wonderful princess doll. Christmas was coming up and Annabelle would so like to have that doll – she had already imagined lots of stories starring the princess.

Yet, at first, Annabelle was disappointed: Mummy dragged the girls straight into a department store with a sale on and treated herself to a new t-shirt. After that, Mummy was feeling rather pleased with herself and so she asked Annabelle, "Well Pet, where would you like to go?"

Annabelle knew this was her opportunity, so she held Mummy's hand very tight and said nervously, "Mummy, could we just look at the princess doll in The Great Toy Store, please, please?"

Reluctantly, Mummy nodded - she had not wanted to return to the shop too soon after the drama of losing Archie last week, but she did not want to disappoint Annabelle. They had all agreed to be very quiet so that, just perhaps, no-one would recognize them. But much to Mummy's embarrassment, the manager spotted them and bellowed from the other side of the store:

"You haven't lost the wee lad already, have you?"

Kate and Mummy blushed. Mummy gave an embarrassed smile and tried to sound jolly as she said, "No, no not this time; we left Archie at home today." The manager laughed and Annabelle dragged Mummy and Kate over to the dolls' section.

It was stunning! There seemed to be dolls of every description: long haired dolls in glittery outfits, bride dolls, baby dolls, talking dolls, walking dolls – Annabelle adored it! She imagined all the dolls she would buy if she were a real princess. Kate had never liked dolls and was rather bored watching Annabelle examine every single doll, so she impatiently blurted out: "For goodness sake Annie, can we look at this princess doll and go and have coffee?"

Annabelle, who had been in her own princess world, snapped back into reality and said in a hurt tone, "I just kind of like to build up to my favourite, special, beautiful, princess doll."

The blow was unexpected – the doll had gone. There was no princess doll. Kate, seeing how disappointed Annabelle was, started to search seriously, moving dolls around all over the place to try and find it. Finally, Mummy intervened: "Sorry Annie, the princess doll has gone. Let's go and get coffee."

In the coffee shop, Annabelle felt close to tears. Mummy held her hand and tried very hard to encourage her. "Who knows. They may get more of the princess dolls. Come on, cheer up Poppet."

Annabelle looked down and tried very hard not to cry. "Sorry Mummy, but I so, so wanted just to look at her. And at Christmas that's all I want. She is just the most lovely princess doll I have ever, ever seen."

Kate patted Annabelle on the head then said sympathetically, "I'm sure Mummy will find you a great present, even if it can't be the princess doll. Or maybe Father Christmas will get his elves to make you one. And anyway, I've made you a fabulous present."

Annabelle couldn't help trying to guess what Kate had made for her and she had almost forgotten the doll when

Mummy ordered two chocolate milkshakes, a coffee and three pastries. Annabelle and Kate both gasped. "Yummy!" The pastries were warm and delicious, and Annabelle savoured every mouthful. She and Kate were both covered in crumbs by the time they'd finished, and Mummy said, "I think you two look so messy now, we'd better leave before we get thrown out."

Annabelle gulped down her last drop of chocolate milkshake, while Kate discussed how much faster she would be able to run with the new trainers they were going to buy. Finally, it was time to go. Kate decisively jumped up and shook the crumbs from her t-shirt onto the floor. An old lady on the next table looked disapprovingly at Kate. Kate grinned and whispered, "I had to Mummy. It's better the floor's covered in crumbs than me." Mummy sighed; Annabelle giggled.

The shoe shop was just a short walk from the coffee shop. Annabelle felt instantly bored surrounded by shoes, but Kate was definitely enjoying herself as she discussed the various trainers with Mummy. In minutes Kate had a pile of boxes in front of her.

Annabelle just knew Kate would take ages choosing which trainers she would have. So Annabelle wandered around aimlessly until she came to a colourful display of slippers. There were red, yellow and green ones; even rainbow-coloured, and pink and mauve glittery slippers. But what really took Annabelle's fancy were the lion slippers. They were gorgeous, just so soft and velvety to stroke. There was a great shaggy lion face at the front, and a sweet little tail at the back and Annabelle felt they would be just like twin puppets on her feet. Annabelle felt she really ought to name the slippers Leo and Lola.

Absorbed in playing with the Leo and Lola, which were now on Annabelle's feet, she had quite forgotten about Kate and the trainers. Mummy's voice seemed abrupt when she called: "Come on Love; we must hurry and get back so Daddy can get Tom to football practice without Archie. And do get those things off your feet."

Annabelle, startled out of her game, clumsily took Leo and Lola off her feet and affectionately said, "Goodbye, I'll come and see you soon."

It was only on the walk home that Annabelle realized that she had lost her opportunity to show her Mum the slippers. It was now that Annabelle understood that, next to the princess doll, she would love to have the lion slippers for Christmas.

Looking up from his castle book, Sam noticed that Annabelle looked rather glum as she came in. Sam was seven years older than Annabelle and had rather a soft spot for his youngest sister. So he enquired: "What's up Annie?" Annabelle explained about the slippers.

Mummy overheard and looked rather guilty: "Sorry I rushed you away from your lion slippers, but honestly Angel I don't really think you would have worn them."

Annabelle knew she would never convince Mummy how different these slippers were to all the other pairs of slippers she had had and never worn – Leo and Lola would be more like friends than just slippers. Sam smiled down at his sister. "Santa is coming soon, so I bet you'll get loads of wonderful presents."

Annabelle looked glum and did one of her best sulky faces. But Mummy had a cunning plan and suggested Annabelle made a marzipan lion, while she put the marzipan on the Christmas cake. Annabelle struggled to stay sulky. She knew Mummy wanted to distract her, but making a marzipan lion did sound fun, so she grinned and said, "Okay, I'd like that if my marzipan lion can go on top of the Christmas cake when you ice it, with the little Father Christmas. And can I have a piece of marzipan to eat?"

Mummy grinned. "Yes we'll both eat just a tiny bit of marzipan as long as you don't tell the others, and yes the lion can join Father Christmas on the cake. It will certainly be quite an unusual Christmas cake!"

Half an hour later, Mummy was laughing as Annabelle placed two marzipan lions either side of the tiny Father Christmas on top of the cake. Chuckling, Annabelle explained: "This one is Lola and this one is Leo and they are Father Christmas' best friends.

CHAPTER 9: EXCITEMENT

Christmas in the Barnes family was an exciting affair: Advent calendars put well out of Archie's way; glittery decorations made at school and pre-school. Of course Kate took control of decorating the Christmas tree: "Archie, we don't want the angel at the bottom of the tree. That tinsel is horrid." Archie was allowed to decorate the back of the tree so Annabelle felt quite important that she was allowed to help Kate decorate the front of the tree.

It was always a very special day when Granny arrived; the Barnes family always said that it properly felt like the Christmas season had begun –with huge hugs and kisses for everyone. This year, Kate thought Granny's cases looked extra full but no-one was allowed to peek into them, even though Annabelle begged and begged to be allowed one tiny look.

Annabelle showed Granny her presents: Tom and Sam had a chocolate bar each; Kate had some hair bands (she was always losing them, plus Annabelle did borrow them quite a lot); Archie had an action figure Annabelle had bought at the school fair and Mummy and Daddy had a photograph in a frame she had made at Pre-school. Naturally, Granny was very impressed: "The presents are gorgeous! Annabelle, you are a very kind and thoughtful girl." Annabelle did have one present she could not show to Granny: the pretty box she had decorated with sequins and glitter; this was for Granny.

There was also a last minute present to buy: Annabelle and Granny rushed into town to buy Rosie's present. As they walked into town, Annabelle explained, "I must give Rosie something very beautiful; you see, Granny, Rosie is my very best friend and we are both princesses."

Granny nodded and then said thoughtfully, "I wonder if a pretty bracelet or hair slides would be right." Annabelle grinned, and in a few minutes Annabelle and Granny were in a rather wonderful, very "girly" shop called Tinsel Town. The crowded shop was dazzling, decorated with silver tinsel and tiny, sparkling fairies.

Annabelle was mesmerized by so much sparkle and glitter, and she whispered, "I'd just so love to buy it all." Finally, it was Granny who spotted the pink glittery hair slides with tiny, tiny, silver fairies on them. Annabelle was thrilled, for she knew Rosie would adore these slides; they were just right for princesses.

Back at home Annabelle and Archie decorated their bedrooms with all the shiny leftover pieces of tinsel that Kate had said were too battered for the living room. Archie loved everything and anything connected with Christmas; like Annabelle, he adored all shiny decoration and jumped up and down each time he spotted a new decoration in a shop. This year Archie understood a little about getting presents at Christmas, so he liked to talk a lot about, "My pres'ts." Happily, Annabelle had found all the Christmas stories – Archie loved his big book with a picture of Father Christmas on it. "My pres'ts, Granny!" he exclaimed, as he showed his Granny a picture of Father Christmas's sack of presents.

Annabelle's favourite Christmas book was one about baby Jesus being born in a stable. Annabelle had seen pictures of herself and her brothers and sister as babies – she understood that it was a very special time when a new baby arrived. It seemed incredible that this most important baby had not had special clothes or a comfortable cot.

Gazing at a picture of Mary, Joseph and baby Jesus in the stable, she whispered to Mummy, "I would love to have held baby Jesus."

Archie joined in the conversation and said, "Me hol' baby." Mummy and Annabelle smiled and Annabelle explained, "Baby Jesus lived a long time ago."

Archie looked confused and Mummy said, "Baby Jesus did live a long time ago, but why don't we go and look at the pretend baby Jesus in our crib set."

Immediately, Archie ran to the window sill where the little wooden crib was displayed and smiled, gazing at the little models. Annabelle thought Archie looked rather "cute" and she was about to hug him when Archie's plump little paw lunged forward to grab the baby Jesus figure. Archie was jolly pleased with himself and, "My baby Jesus."

Annabelle was appalled. "You are so naughty, Archie!"

Fortunately, Mummy acted quickly: she gently squeezed his little hand and said, "Let's leave the baby there to help

us all remember about baby Jesus."

Archie nodded and looked up at Mummy: "Annabelle mus' no' tush."

Mummy grinned at Annabelle. "No, Annabelle mustn't touch." Annabelle tried to frown at Archie but she couldn't help herself giggling.

The living room door burst open and Kate rushed in: "Everyone into the kitchen; we're going to light the Advent candle." Daddy lit the Advent candle; Sam turned off the light and the candle burned brightly.

Archie whispered, "Me ha'."

Daddy grinned and put the candle on a high shelf: "I don't think so, but you and Annie can blow it out." As the family watched the flickering flame, Annabelle thought about baby Jesus. Then Annabelle and Archie blew as hard as they could.

When Archie gloated, "Me blow not Ann!" Annabelle decided just this once she wouldn't say anything; after all, she and Sam knew Annabelle had blown the candle out, so Annabelle and Sam just grinned at each other.

It seemed strange that, even on Christmas Eve, Mummy should be saying, "Come on! Bath and bed."

Excitedly, Kate interrupted, "They can't go to bed! Annie and I are going to wrap prezzies." Annabelle grinned. Kate had promised to help her do her wrapping up so that her presents looked really beautiful.

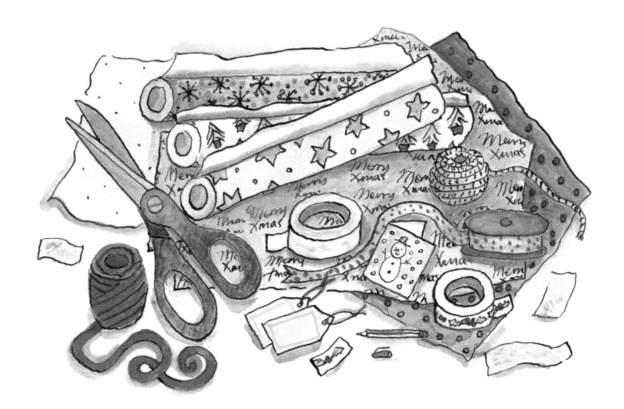

Archie was a little confused, but one thing he did know was that he didn't want to go to bed, so he was rather pleased when Granny said, "Come on Archie, come and help Granny; I've got some lovely paper."

However, it was not long before Mummy shouted upstairs, "Archie, Annabelle, we really must get you two off to bed – come for stories."

As the two children raced into the living room, Daddy shook his head: "Instead of story tonight, I've got a special job for Archie and Annabelle. You need to put out a mince pie and a glass of sherry for Father Christmas." Annabelle and Archie both felt so excited and even Tom wanted to help. In fact, it was Tom who remembered the reindeer.

Sam smiled. "I hope we've got lots of carrots 'cause Father Christmas has at least six reindeer and I think they'll all be very hungry."

Annabelle retorted, "Reindeer are very good at sharing and don't eat a lot when they're working." Do you know, Daddy felt sure Annabelle was right, which was just as well, because there were only three carrots in the fridge. Daddy had forgotten to buy the carrots.

Finally, Tom and Kate ran noisily downstairs, yelling, "Emergency, emergency, we almost forgot the stockings." Each child had their own special place to put their stocking. Sam and Kate fell out over this; both believed that their stocking went next to the sofa near the window. Annabelle managed to sort it out by begging Sam to bring his stocking

next to hers. Archie found it difficult to let go of his stocking and kept spinning round: "Fa' Chris' prese' me!" Daddy picked both Archie and Annabelle up, putting the stocking down, and rather solemnly explained that Father Christmas only came to good children who went to bed nicely on Christmas Eve.

It had been a tiring day and, though Annabelle had hoped to get a glimpse of Father Christmas, she found herself drifting off to sleep almost as soon as she snuggled down, just aware of Archie's peaceful, heavy breathing.

CHAPTER 10: Christmas Morning

It was five o'clock on Christmas morning and Tom was running madly around the house yelling, "He's been! Come on everyone, get up!"

Daddy was the first to get up and he didn't seem quite as excited as Tom: Daddy spoke in a very firm, controlled voice, "No-one is getting up yet – this is the middle of the night and Mummy and Daddy need to sleep."

Tom grumbled but quietened down, left Archie fast asleep in his bedroom, and went into Annabelle's room.

Annabelle was just so, so wide awake. "Has Santa really been? Has he even filled Archie's sack?" Annabelle knew that quite often Archie wasn't a good boy and she had been a little worried that Santa might not feel he deserved any presents. Annabelle went and looked over at Archie with his pink cheeks and short blond curls, tightly cuddling his teddy, and thought how upset he would be if he had no presents.

Tom whispered excitedly, "There are loads and loads of presents. My sack looks massive." Tom told Annabelle in great detail about all the presents he was hoping for, many related to football. Annabelle thought it would be all right to give Tom his present a bit early, especially as she felt sure he'd let her have a bite of the chocolate bar. Tom tore the wrapping off, looked at his sister, grinned teasingly, then let Annabelle have a bite. Moments later, Tom appeared with rather a scrumpled small parcel. "This is for you; I wrapped it myself." It was a pink ribbon and Annabelle felt sure it would be very pretty, once all the crumples had fallen out. Tom looked very proud of himself: it had not been easy for him choosing a ribbon for Annabelle.

Six thirty and Archie woke up and was immediately very excited and very loud. Tom grinned mischievously at Annabelle, and then said sweetly to Archie, "Why don't you check if Mummy and Daddy are awake?"

Archie ran into his parents' room yelling, "It's Chrismuss, Chrismuss ! Prezzies me, prezzies me!"

Tom grinned, as Mummy and Daddy emerged bleary-eyed from the bedroom. Annabelle kissed Kate and Granny awake, and Archie jumped on Sam. Yet even after all Archie's efforts, Daddy insisted that he, Mummy and

Granny had a coffee before they attacked the presents. I'm not sure it was a very relaxing coffee: Tom teased Archie. "You're far too naughty to get prezzies."

Archie screamed, "Me goo'!" And poor Annabelle worried: she could remember a lot of times when indeed Archie had not been good.

Finally, after what seemed like years, slowly, ever so slowly, Daddy inched the living room door open, whispering, "Do you know I'm not sure Santa has visited us." This was too much for Tom who flung himself past Daddy and leapt into the living room to feast his eyes on the heaps of presents.

Following Tom, Archie squeezed into the room to immediately let out a wail, "Where my? Where my?" He grabbed greedily and wildly at several stockings, which the other children heaved protectively to their chests.

Kate picked Archie up and, chuckling, exclaimed, "We'll find your stocking!" Annabelle remembered the many naughty things Archie did daily and did not feel so hopeful, yet to her own surprise it was she who spotted Archie's stocking, bulging with presents. In a very grown up princess voice, Annabelle explained how lucky Archie was to have presents this year.

I'm not sure Archie really heard much of what Annabelle was saying, though he did hug her and kiss her and generously announce reassuringly, "Annboo ha' pres' too." Annabelle felt a bit irritated with Archie: of course she would get presents; she was a good girl. I think Mummy understood a little of what Annabelle was feeling, as she grinned and handed Annabelle her stocking. Annabelle smiled, for it's difficult to feel even the tiniest bit grumpy when you have a stocking full of wonderful presents in front of you.

Amidst all the chaos of the unwrapping frenzy, Annabelle looked round the room: Santa had remembered everyone and Annabelle felt just so happy that she said a little thank you prayer to Jesus. Daddy, who had noticed that Annabelle was sitting quietly for a moment, came to check that she was all right and also, of course, he wanted to have a peek at her presents.

Annabelle sat on Daddy's knee and confided, "Isn't having prezzies a great way to remember that baby Jesus was born on Christmas day."

Daddy kissed her and said, "It is fun isn't it? Though, do you know, just sometimes I wish Archie could enjoy himself without making quite so much noise." Daddy and Annabelle chuckled, while Archie jumped up and down and shrieked with excitement.

For almost quarter of an hour the children were wholly

absorbed in attacking the piles of presents from Father

Christmas. Archie was still attempting to work a traction engine truck, with half his stocking unopened. Annabelle had offered to finish the unwrapping, but Mummy felt this might well cause offence, so she suggested Annabelle hand out her presents. Granny was thrilled with her beautifully decorated box, and Sam liked his chocolate bar and gobbled it up while examining his book on knights. Kate said that the new hair bands would be jolly useful and she thought she could just about cope with the one pink one. Archie used his new action figure to attack a toy car, so Annabelle guessed that that meant he liked it. Of course Mummy and Daddy were delighted with the lovely photo frame Annabelle had made for them.

Enthusiastically, Kate flung her presents at everyone. Annabelle very carefully unwrapped the pretty paper to reveal a lovely glittery necklace that Kate had made for her. Kate smiled. "I knew you would love it; I chose as many pink, glittery beads as I could afford."

Before Archie could become too interested in the necklace, Granny handed him a large parcel, then tuned to Annabelle: "Well Annabelle, I took a bit of advice from Mummy, so I hope you like them." Annabelle could not believe her eyes when she saw, beneath the shiny wrapping paper, the lion slippers she wanted. Annabelle jumped on Granny to hug her, and cried, "Now I have these, I don't want anything else!"

Mummy grinned. "Well that is a shame! What will I do with this present?" Annabelle jumped up and down and begged her Mummy to let her have it. Mummy whispered loudly to Daddy, "What do you think?" Kate grabbed the present and threw it to Annabelle: "You have Archie to thank for this. Mum threatened to bring Archie back into the toy shop if they didn't order another one for you." Annabelle tore at the paper to find the beautiful princess doll she so wanted. Annabelle glowed with happiness.

Even Sam put down his castle book and admired the splendid new doll. Poor Archie was rather dazzled by its gorgeous golden hair. His truck no longer seemed so special, and he looked pleadingly at Annabelle and said, "Me share."

Annabelle calmly shook her head. Fortunately, Kate, sensing trouble, picked Archie up and tickled him: " No way Archie!" and both Archie and Annabelle chuckled delightedly. Annabelle struggled for a moment, then said, "I just can't share my beautiful doll, but I will share my slippers." Archie looked at the great, golden, furry lion slippers and grinned, shouting, "Mine! Mine!" Sam quickly asked Archie, "What will you call Annieboo's slippers?" Annabelle felt just too happy to be cross with Sam for calling her Annieboo.

Sam pretended to be serious: "Leo and Lola are boring names – how about Naboo and Prune?" Annabelle ignored her brother: he always liked reminding her of these horrible nicknames. But Archie nodded vigorously.

That night, after wonderful food and far too many chocolates, Archie and Annabelle collapsed into bed. Annabelle sat her beautiful doll, Princess Rosie, on her bedside table, dreaming of all the new princess clothes

Mummy could make for her. Archie too was peaceful, fast asleep clutching the lion slippers that he so loved. After all, Mummy had been right about the slippers -Annabelle never did wear them. Archie adored them and he would certainly never allow Annabelle to wear Naboo Lion and Prune Lion, his new friends.

FROM THE AUTHOR

I love children; as mother to seven children I suppose that is fairly obvious. For the last twenty-three years my life has very much been centred round children. Additionally, I now work in a play group and have loved spending time with other people's gorgeous children. One of my favourite things as a Mum of a young child was to sit and read stories with them; it was such a lovely cosy time.

Books that my daughters particularly enjoyed were "My Naughty Little Sister," and "Milly Molly Mandy." Incidentally, these were books that I too had loved reading as a child and so they were definitely a key inspiration. I wanted to write a book celebrating and just enjoying the little incidents that make up a child's life and I loosely based the characters on my own children as they were growing up. It seems to me that childhood should ideally be a safe, joyful time and I wanted to write a book that created this sort of world.

FROM THE ILLUSTRATOR

I studied Art on the Foundation course at Medway College of Art and Design; then went on to study Graphic Design at Canterbury Art College (now UCA). I am a freelance illustrator; hand painting china and illustrating books, as well as taking on one-off commissions. It has been a delight illustrating Debbie's book. Entering into a child's view of the world is always my favourite thing!

ABOUT JENGA

Jenga Community Development Outreach is a Christian non-profit charity based in Uganda, East Africa. They're a longstanding, locally trusted organisation made up of national employees and international volunteers working together to make a difference.

They supply villages with clean water and train women to save and wisely invest their money. They give goats to widows and provide vocational training to vulnerable single mothers. They pray with prison inmates and sponsor kids to attend school. The projects are diverse and their presence is widespread.

Some of the proceeds from the sale of 'Princess Annabelle' will go towards Jenga's projects in Uganda.

Lightning Source UK Ltd.
Milton Keynes UK
UKOW07n2342161117
312856UK00003B/27/P

9 781999 746407